Katherine Applegate

Doggo AND Pupper

SAVE THE WORLD

illustrated by **Charlie Alder**

Feiwel and Friends

New York

For Amy Goldsmith, with love.

—KA

For my lovely Mum, and—always—J & W.

—CA

A Feiwel and Friends Book
An imprint of Macmillan Publishing Group, LLC
120 Broadway, New York, NY 10271
mackids.com

Library of Congress Cataloging-in-Publication Data is available.

First edition, 2022
Book design by Liz Dresner
Feiwel and Friends logo designed by Filomena Tuosto
The artist used a combination of collage and digital
techniques to create the illustrations for this book.
Printed in China by RR Donnelley Asia Printing Solutions Ltd.,
Dongguan City, Guangdong Province

ISBN 978-1-250-62100-9 (hardcover)
1 3 5 7 9 10 8 6 4 2

Contents

Chapter One

Wonderful

In a sweet spot of sun,
Doggo dozed.
    In a fine patch of dirt,
Pupper dug.
    Life was good.

A little bird flew by.
Her soft nest held two babies.
"Soon they will fly," said Doggo.

"I wish I could fly like that bird," said
Pupper. "Or like Wonder Dog."
"I have not met that fellow," said Doggo.
"He is on TV," said Pupper. "He is not
afraid of anything. Even giant squirrels."

Pupper worried
a lot about giant
squirrels.

"I will never be a hero," said Pupper.
"I worry too much."
    "Even heroes worry," said Doggo.
    "Do cats worry?" Pupper asked Cat.
    "No," she said. "It is a waste of time.
We also do not fly."

"Pupper, you do not need to fly like Wonder Dog," said Doggo. "You are already wonderful."

Chapter Two

Hero

"We are going to the movies," said the humans. "Be good, pets."

Doggo found the zapper.

The humans laughed. "Sure," they said. "Watch TV! Good luck finding shows to see."

Cat made popcorn.
Pupper picked a show.
It was called *Wonder Dog
Saves the World.*

"I want to be a hero," said Pupper. "But I need someone to save. Do you need any saving, Cat?"

"Not at this time," said Cat.
"But thank you for asking."

Doggo picked the next show.
It had loud music. Cat covered
her ears.

"When I was a pup, I was in a rock band," said Doggo. "It was called The Beagles."

"Is that so," said Cat.

"I played the drums," said Doggo.

"Would you teach me to play the drums?" Pupper asked.

Doggo gave Pupper two spoons.

"Lesson one," he said. "Drumming is hard work."

"Oh," said Pupper. "Then I would rather be a hero."

Doggo smiled. "That is hard work, too," he said.

Chapter Three

Drumming

Pupper drummed
all night.

He drummed
all day.

He drummed all week.

26

"Do you like my music, Cat?" he asked.
"There are many kinds of music," said Cat.
"I like the quiet kind."

"Great news!" said Doggo. "Tomorrow there will be music in the park. A band is going to play."

"Will they have drums?" asked Pupper.
"Every good band has drums," said
Doggo.

A baby bird flew past.

"Look!" said Pupper. "She is learning how to fly."

The other baby was still in the nest.

"I wonder if he is scared," said Pupper.

"He will fly when he is ready," said Doggo.

"Maybe he is worried about giant squirrels," said Pupper.

"Maybe he just needs some peace and quiet," said Cat.

Chapter Four

Chirp Chirp Chirp!

Pupper could not wait to hear the band.
At last it was time to go.
"Hurry, Doggo!" he called.

"Cat, are you coming?" asked Doggo.

"It is my nap time," said Cat.

"It is always your nap time," said Doggo.

"Napping is my only job," said Cat. "But I do it well."

Doggo and Pupper started out.
Flit! Flap! Zoom!
The mother bird zipped over them.
One baby followed her.

"I wish I could be that quick," said Doggo. "But these days I am slow."

"I am fast," said Pupper.
"Stay near," said Doggo.
"Or I will worry."

"You worry, too?"
Pupper asked.
    "Only about
important things,"
said Doggo.

They turned a corner.
The breeze was soft.

It smelled like ice cream.
It held happy voices.

Pupper heard a
new sound.

A tiny *chirp chirp chirp!*

Something was under a bush.

Did giant squirrels
live under bushes?

Chirp chirp chirp!
It was a scared sound.
Not a scary one.

Pupper peeked.

Under the bush was a tiny
bird. He looked very worried.

Chapter Five

The Baby Bird

"Are you all right, baby bird?"
Pupper asked.

The baby blinked.
Chirp chirp chirp!

"Doggo!" Pupper called.
"Come here!"

"Well, look at that!" said
Doggo. "The other baby."

"Why is he all alone?"
asked Pupper.

"He is called a fledgling," said Doggo. "He is learning how to fly. But his mother is nearby."
"I cannot just leave him here," said Pupper.

"The music is about to start," said Doggo.

"I know," said Pupper. "But he might be worried about giant squirrels."

Chirp chirp chirp! said the baby.

"Someone needs to save this bird,"
said Pupper. "And I am that someone."

Chapter Six

Waiting

Doggo and Pupper sat near the bush.

They were close
to the baby bird.
But not too close.

They waited.

They were quiet as clouds.
The breeze carried new sounds.

The band was playing.

Pupper heard drums.
"We could still go," said Doggo.

"Wonder Dog would not leave,"
said Pupper.

73

The baby bird flapped his wings.

He hopped.

74

But he did
not fly.

They waited and
waited and waited.
The band stopped
playing.

"I am sorry we missed the music,"
said Pupper.
"There will be other bands,"
said Doggo.

Swoop!

The mother bird flew
down. The other bird
followed her.

They all chirped.

They all flapped.

They all hopped.

And then, at last,
they all flew.

81

Chapter Seven

Music

Doggo and Pupper watched the birds fly high.

They sat quietly.

They listened to the sounds of the day.

Bees buzzed.
Leaves fluttered.

Squirrels chittered.

They were not the
giant kind.
"Cat was right," said
Doggo. "There are many
kinds of music."

Pupper found
some sticks.

He and Doggo
drummed along
with the day.

They made a
fine band.

Finally, they
walked home.

The birds were
waiting in a tree.
"I still want to be
a hero like Wonder
Dog," said Pupper.
Chirp chirp chirp!
said the birds.

"You are off to a very good start,"
said Doggo.

Pupper's Guide to Being a Hero

Be **helpful**.

Imagine how others feel.

Listen well.

Be a **friend**.

Don't give up.

Try **kindness**.

Share what you have.

Stay **safe**.

 **Shake** things off.

Make someone **smile**.